D1483250

Dreary & Naughty

The Misadventures of Dreary & Naughty

John LaFleur
&
Shawn Dubin

Other Schiffer Books by the Author:

Dreary & Naughty: Friday the 13th of February,
978-07643-4495-4, $14.99

Dreary & Naughty: The ABCs of Being Dead,
978-07643-44961, $14.99

Library of Congress Control Number: 2013941028

Designed by John P. Cheek
Type set in Sandra Oh

ISBN: 978-07643-44947
Printed in China

Published by Schiffer Publishing, Ltd.
4880 Lower Valley Road
Atglen, PA 19310
Phone: (610) 5931777; Fax: (610) 593-2002
E-mail: Info@schifferbooks.com

For our complete selection of fine books on this and related subjects, please visit our website at www.schifferbooks.com. You may also write for a free catalog.

This book may be purchased from the publisher. Please try your bookstore first.

We are always looking for people to write books on new and related subjects. If you have an idea for a book, please contact us at proposals@schifferbooks.com

Schiffer Publishing's titles are available at special discounts for bulk purchases for sales promotions or premiums. Special editions, including personalized covers, corporate imprints, and excerpts can be created in large quantities for special needs. For more information, contact the publisher.

For The Believers: Gino, Pat, Tom, Shawn, and Trish
–John

For Mom and everyone that made this possible
–Shawn

Dreary and Naughty weren't two of a kind.
Two more opposite friends, one could never find.

Dreary was bony and chalky and grim.
Naughty was pretty and sassy and slim.

The two friends attended a regular school,
Where Naughty left all the boys dripping with drool.

The girls they found Dreary a bit of a ghoul.
He accidentally scared them all into the pool.

Naughty intimidated the girl's self-esteem.
As to being more like her, they could only dream.

Her bangles bore inscriptions
Of words clever woven,
Her boots covered feet
Of hooves that were cloven.

Her smile was quite brilliant,
Her teeth were bright white.
The boys always tried
To keep her in sight.

She was a bit different,
With her tiny short tail,
But it looked good on her;
She was thin as a rail.

Dreary simply brought
All the boys down.
When he'd come by
They would simply frown.

He tried to dress like them
And bought all their clothes,
But he preferred ones
Where the bones always showed.

When it came to fashion
And trying to look cool,
He had just one idiom
Always saying, "skulls rule."

So sometimes he passed
As a very cool kid;
More often than not though,
That's not what he did.

School was a drag.
It never went well.
Both of them saw it
A small slice of hell.

They'd often share classes,
But sometimes they'd not.
On those lonely days,
They'd catch up at their spot.

Everyday they'd connect,
To partake in a lunch,
And joke about mystery meat
That sometimes went "crunch."

All through their schedule,
Around the hall's bend,
They stuck by each other
Until the day's end.

Most of the kids
Would just point and stare.
Neither of them seemed
To notice or care.

The pair had each other,
And thankfully so,
For else they'd be lonely
Where ever they'd go.

On the way home,
Together they'd walk.
Sometimes they said nothing,
And sometimes they'd talk

No one lived near them,
Normal kids weren't around.
Their cadaverous home:
The Dark Side of Town.

Dreary's house was all white,
Made sturdily of bone.
The walls were all plastered
With rows of gravestone.

Naughty's home was bright red
With windows of skin.
Its walls were of fire,
The roof of hot tin.

Dreary had parents,
Who looked much like him;
Both similarly skeletal
And terribly thin.

Naughty: she had
Both a mom and a dad,
And though they were evil
They always looked glad.

Despite their appearance,
The folks loved their kid,
So when they got home
They'd ask what they did.

Both of the friends
Told their parents of gym,
And attempted performances,
Which were often quite grim.

Dreary was fragile –
Not much of a runner.
When checked during rough play,
It was often a bummer.

As Dreary was injured,
The other kids scoffed.
The coach just looked down
And said, "Walk it off."

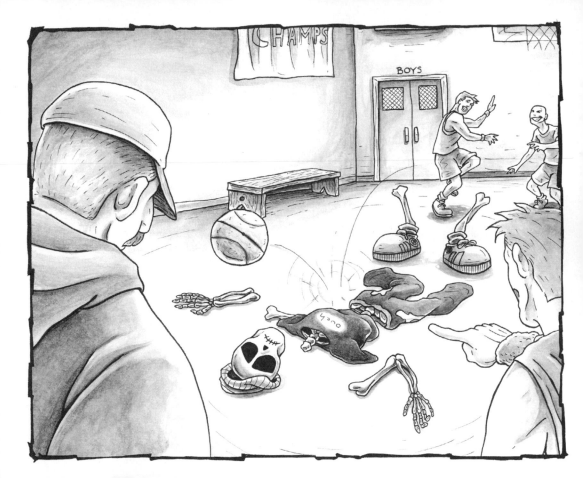

By school regulation,
Naughty was forced to play,
So when she'd tend goal
She'd stop it her way.

Once they were home,
They'd talk on the phone
From up in their rooms.
They were never alone.

They'd chat and they'd speak,
Long into the night,
About how school was awful,
How the kids weren't all right.

They'd contemplate ways
To both stay home sick,
And thought up excuses
Their parents would pick.

Dreary tried often,
The fake sick routine;
He'd point to his jawbone
Or his missing spleen.

On the days that he'd try
To not go to school,
It never did work,
His mom was no fool.

He'd plead for a bit,
To try and stay in.
His parents said no
With a white toothy grin.

"Why can't I be home-schooled?
Why can't I learn here?
Why must I go
To where all the kids jeer?"

His dad said, "Buck up."
His mom gave him cheers.
They sent him along,
To learn with his "peers."

Naughty tried also
To pass her fake ills.
Instead of a fever,
She'd complain of the chills.

Her Pop soon caught on:
She was being a liar,
And filled her right up
With a shot full of fire.

While Dreary and Naughty
Were forced to attend,
The other kids' opinions,
They just could not bend.

"These two, they are different;
This pair, they aren't cool."
Or so it was said,
By the kids in the school.

"The boy is a monster."
"The girl is one, too."
"They both really scare us."
"So, what shall we do?"

They talked and they plotted,
Well into the night,
About the odd pair,
That gave them such fright.

And so those mean kids
All hatched up a threat;
They connived and they whispered
To relieve their fret.

When it was morning,
Came the dawn with a plan.
They'd finished their scheme,
And soon it began.

That very next day,
When no one was looking,
They captured the duo
And got their plan cooking.

Fear filled each stomach,
Hate blackened each heart,
And so they took action,
That was not very smart.

"The boy must be buried,
The girl must be burned.
They're just too darn weird,
And so they are spurned."

"Get them, they're different."
"I think this one's dead!"
"That girl's got horns
Coming out of her head."

"They're just not like us.
They sure don't fit in.
We're all afraid
Of her confident grin."

They buried the boy
Made of fragile bone,
Alongside the girl,
Who smelled of brimstone.

Dreary and Naughty
Were nowhere to be found.
No smart-ass remarks,
No sad mellow sound.

So, when school did end,
And the pair didn't come home,
The Dark Side of Town
Let their sentiment known.

Those mean kids—they got theirs.
The two were *not* dead,
Their parents did miss them,
And got angry instead.

Calling on minions
Of fire and bone,
They dug up their children,
And brought them both home.

The following events
All did make the news,
As the mean kids' folks
Had epitaphs to choose.

The boys and the girls
From this world disappeared,
Victims of parents
Of those they most feared.

Obituaries read
Were often quite gruesome,
And echoed of themes
By our fearful young twosome.

Freshly dug graves
Were soon in abundance,
And scripted the tales
Of the bullies' comeuppance.

So what can be learned?
What does resonate?
Which moral will stay?
To make you feel great?

Don't ostracize those
Who are not like you;
Accept them with kindness
Is what you should do.

For one never knows
From the cover of a book,
What lies deep inside,
So take time for a look.

What more can be said,
To save you your breath....

*Don't pick on the children
Of the Devil and Death.*

Deadicated to
the misunderstood, the
under-appreciated, the confused,
the troubled, the anxiety ridden,
the overlooked, and the
lonely everywhere

About the Authors

John LaFleur grew up face first in the ten volumes of Collier's *The Junior Classics*, spending far too much time in the Mythology and Folk Tales volumes. He lives in Elgin, Illinois, with his wife Trish, son Morgan, and an assortment of indoor/outdoor cats. He enjoys creating children's and young adult stories in the footsteps of the writers who inspired him as a child.

Shawn Dubin spent much of his time growing up immersed in comic books and watching creature double features on Saturday afternoons. Currently he resides in Philadelphia, Pennsylvania, with his wife and their brood of cats. Shawn has been drawing since he could first hold a writing implement and will most likely die drawing.

About the Book

The Misadventures of Dreary and Naughty introduces two new icons to the world of children's and teen literature. In a world where everyday is Halloween, this is a cautionary tale about the son of the Grim Reaper (Dreary) and the daughter of the Devil (Naughty), who are sent by their parents to attend high school with mortal children to learn about humanity—and how "inhuman" high school years can be. Set in verse by John LaFleur and illustrated in black and white watercolor by Shawn Dubin, it is a story that reminds both young and old how it feels to be ostracized during our sometimes-challenging school years. Embedded in the story is a gentle reminder of the importance of tolerance and true friendship, and how both can make school days go a little easier. This brand new edition marks the 10-year anniversary of the title's initial release in 2003 and features some revised text from the original.